What Else Can I Play?
Flute
Grade Two

Series Editor: Mark Mumford

Music arranged and processed by
Barnes Music Engraving Ltd
East Sussex TN22 4HA, England

Published 1995

Introduction

In this *What Else Can I Play?* collection you'll find sixteen popular tunes that are both challenging and entertaining.

The pieces have been carefully selected and arranged to create ideal supplementary material for young flautists who are either working towards or have recently taken a Grade Two flute examination.

Technical demands increase progressively, gradually introducing new concepts that reflect the requirements of the major examination boards. Each piece offers suggestions and guidelines on breathing, dynamics and tempo, together with technical tips and performance notes.

Pupils will experience a wide variety of music, ranging from folk and classical through to showtunes and popular songs, leading to a greater awareness of musical styles.

Whether it's for light relief from examination preparation, or to reinforce the understanding of new concepts, this collection will enthuse and encourage all young flute players.

Note: references to fingering within this book use Thumb 1 2 3 4.

Scarborough fair

Traditional

The sun has got his hat on

Words and Music by Ralph Butler and Noel Gay

The teddy bears' picnic

Words by Jimmy Kennedy, Music by John Bratton

Do-Re-Mi

Words by Oscar Hammerstein II, Music by Richard Rodgers

Miss Marple

Ken Howard and Alan Blaikley

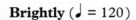

Que sera, sera
(Whatever will be, will be)

Words and Music by Jay Livingston and Ray Evans

Last of the summer wine

Ronnie Hazlehurst

What shall we do with the drunken sailor?

Traditional

Moderately ($\quad$ = 112)

What Else Can I Play?
Flute
Grade Two

Scarborough fair

Traditional

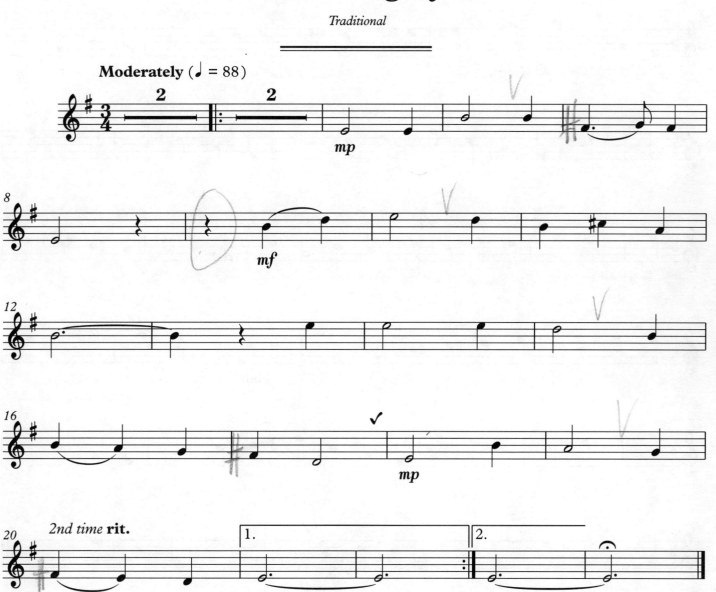

This old English folk-song once appeared in the pop charts in an arrangement by American singing duo Simon and Garfunkel, who, earlier in their careers, performed under the 'borrowed' title *Tom and Jerry*.

If you think of always aiming for the first beat of each bar it will help shape the four bar phrases in this tune. Try to produce a warm, well-rounded tone for the lower notes.

The sun has got his hat on

Words and Music by Ralph Butler and Noel Gay

This 1930s song was very popular during the Second World War and received a surprise hit revival in the 1960s from a group called The Temperance Seven.

Keep the crotchets nice and bouncy to create a jolly sound but be sure to hold the dotted minims for their full value. The time signature is ₵ i.e. two minims in a bar. At first you may find it to easier to count this as four crotchets but then try to establish a 'one-and-two-and' count, to get that two-in-a-bar feel.

The teddy bears' picnic

Words by Jimmy Kennedy, Music by John Bratton

This famous children's song was written in 1907. However, it was made most popular by Henry Hall and his orchestra in the 1930s. Hall was an accomplished bandleader who directed the BBC Dance Orchestra.

Give the opening of this piece a 'misterioso' atmosphere by keeping the quavers short and observing the gradually increasing dynamics. To help with the fingering in bar 9, practise playing D to E, slowly, several times (don't forget to remove your right hand little finger when playing D!).

Do-Re-Mi

Words by Oscar Hammerstein II, Music by Richard Rodgers

This is one of the most famous songs from Rodgers and Hammerstein's 1959 musical, *The Sound Of Music*. Do, Re and Mi are the first three notes of the major scale. This system of naming notes is called tonic sol-fa. It was developed by Sarah Glover in the early nineteenth century and later adapted by John Curwen.

Here's a chance for you to show off if you've been practising your scales, because that's what this piece is all about! Don't forget to keep your left hand first finger off for the E flat (D sharp) in bar 30 and make sure that you hold the tied notes for their full value.

Miss Marple

Ken Howard and Alan Blaikley

The character of Miss Marple was originally created by detective novelist Dame Agatha Christie (1890–1976) who also created the famous Belgian investigator Hercule Poirot.

There is a danger in this piece that the high notes will dominate the phrases, so make sure that you play all notes with an equally strong tone. The tenuto marks – and accents > of the middle section should be carefully observed to make the music more interesting and expressive.

Que sera, sera
(Whatever will be, will be)

Words and Music by Jay Livingston and Ray Evans

This song is from Alfred Hitchcock's re-make of his own film *The Man Who Knew Too Much*. Made in 1956 it was the second version, starring James Stewart and Doris Day, which that year won the Academy Award for Best Song.

The time signature tells you to count in three, but when you feel you know the music well enough, experiment with counting just one in a bar. This can help to create a more swinging waltz style. To prevent the long note at the end going flat, turn your flute out and raise the airstream as you diminuendo.

Last of the summer wine

Ronnie Hazlehurst

Ronnie Hazlehurst, who composed this theme for Roy Clarke's popular television comedy series, also wrote theme tunes for *Blankety Blank*, *Sorry!* and many others. He became Head Of Music for Television Light Entertainment at the BBC.

To keep the mood of this piece tranquil, play the phrases nice and gently, using legato tonguing. The quaver D in bar 18 may be quite difficult to play *mezzo forte*, so practise some low notes and try to make them 'speak' straight away.

What shall we do with the drunken sailor?

Traditional

A traditional sea shanty, the rhythm of this working song would help to co-ordinate the team efforts of a ship's crew in hoisting sails and other heavy tasks.

The articulation should help you achieve the necessary 'bounce'. In the first section, keep the staccatos short and really emphasise the accented notes. Play the second section with a bold and confident tone.

Green grow the rashes O'

Robert Burns

With bounce (♩ = 92)

This lusty song is by the Scottish poet Robert Burns (1759–1796) who declares that, above all other worldly pleasures, his sweetest hours are 'spent among the lasses, O''.

Before you play this on your flute, first make sure that you can clap the dotted rhythms which occur several times throughout the piece. Also take care to count the rests in the first time bar, just before the repeat.

Mairzy doats and dozy doats

Words and Music by Milton Drake, Al Hoffman and Jerry Livingston

The title of this tune is a play on the words of the song, which tell us that 'Mares eat oats and does eat oats and little lambs eat ivy'.

Make this music sound light and bouncy, especially the dotted crotchets in the middle section, and see if you can create the feeling of a country jig. The melody covers a fairly wide range so be careful to keep the dynamic level even. In particular, avoid allowing the low notes to sound much more quietly than the high notes.

Gavotte

Giovanni Martini

A Gavotte is a dance which, along with several other popular dances from the French countryside, became fashionable in courtly circles in the sixteenth century. It is believed that this piece was composed by Giovanni Martini (1706–1784) although there was another Giovanni Martini (1741–1816). The later Martini pretended to be Italian but was actually a German whose real name was Johann Paul Aegidius Schwartzendorf. He wrote *Plaisir D'Amour* (which is French!).

This should be a lively piece, offering plenty of expressive detail. Take care to observe the articulation marks and don't be put off by the piano accompaniment! Watch out for the fact that the note E sounds twice in bar 5.

© 1995 International Music Publications Limited, Woodford Green, Essex IG8 8HN

The green leaves of summer

Words by Paul Francis Webster, Music by Dimitri Tiomkin

The music for this song was written by Dimitri Tiomkin (1894–1979) who was a Russian-American composer and pianist. As well as composing many film scores Tiomkin performed the European première of George Gershwin's Piano Concerto in F.

Think about the rhythm of the second bar before playing it and make sure that you have a good left hand position for the G sharp (keeping your third and fourth fingers curved). In bar 16 be careful not to let the note B sound sharp as you crescendo. Try to produce a strong, singing tone throughout but especially for the high point of the tune at bar 9.

That's amore

Words by Jack Brooks, Music by Harry Warren

This song comes from the 1953 film *The Caddy* starring Dean Martin, Jerry Lewis and Donna Reed, in which Lewis plays a budding professional golfer who is afraid of crowds. It became Dean Martin's theme song.

Look carefully at the dynamics in bars 20 to 34. Remember that you must come down from *forte* to *mezzo piano* to be able to crescendo again. This piece in the key of D major, so don't forget your C sharps!

When the red, red robin comes bob, bob, bobbin' along

Words and Music by Harry Woods

This song appears in Alfred E. Green's 1946 film *The Jolson Story* starring Larry Parks and Evelyn Keyes. Al Jolson was a theatrical singer of extraordinary reputation, billed for many years as 'America's Greatest Entertainer'. He starred in the first ever 'talkie' picture *The Jazz Singer*, which was made as a joint venture with the Warner Brothers company in 1927. The film's huge success changed the company's fortunes and revolutionised the film industry.

This cheerful tune requires a bright, vibrant performance. Make the staccato notes bouncy but not too short. A good curved left hand position and use of your Thumb B flat key will help make bars 27 and 28 easier to play.

The piper o' Dundee

Traditional

The Piper O'Dundee 'played a spring, the laird to please', a spring in this context, being a quick, lively tune played on the bagpipes. The laird would be the local landlord. This traditional Scottish song has been recorded by numerous artists, Ewan MacColl and Kenneth McKellar among them.

Where there are two quavers slurred it often makes musical sense to 'lean' slightly on the first of the pair. Doing so in this tune will help to give those phrases a good clear start. Use strong tonguing to give the dotted rhythms more impact.

Wouldn't it be loverly

Words by Alan Jay Lerner, Music by Frederick Loewe

This song is from Lerner and Loewe's 1956 musical *My Fair Lady*. The show is based on a play by George Bernard Shaw, called *Pygmalion*. In 1964 it was made into a film, starring Audrey Hepburn and Rex Harrison, which was highly successful and won several Oscars.

This piece is an interesting sequence of bold and wistful phrases. Try to really swing the rhythms in bars 20 and 26 making sure that you play the triplet quavers equally and not as ♫♫. Towards the end, as you play more slowly and quietly, try also to change the tone to a softer, more legato sound.

Green grow the rashes O'

Robert Burns

Mairzy doats and dozy doats

Words and Music by Milton Drake, Al Hoffman and Jerry Livingston

Gavotte

Giovanni Martini

The green leaves of summer

Words by Paul Francis Webster, Music by Dimitri Tiomkin

That's amore

Words by Jack Brooks, Music by Harry Warren

When the red, red robin comes bob, bob, bobbin' along

Words and Music by Harry Woods

The piper o' Dundee

Traditional

Moderately (♩ = 80)

Wouldn't it be loverly

Words by Alan Jay Lerner, Music by Frederick Loewe

rit. poco a poco